A, B, C
ANIMALS
ILLUSTRATED BY TOKO HOSOYA

Designed by Flowerpot Press
in Franklin, TN.
www.FlowerpotPress.com
Designer: Stephanie Meyers
Editor: Ashley Rideout
DJS-0912-0140
ISBN: 978-1-4867-0859-8
Made in China/Fabriqué en Chine

Let's all say our A, B, C's!

Alligator

Bear

Cat

uck

Elephant

FOX

Giraffe

Hedgehog

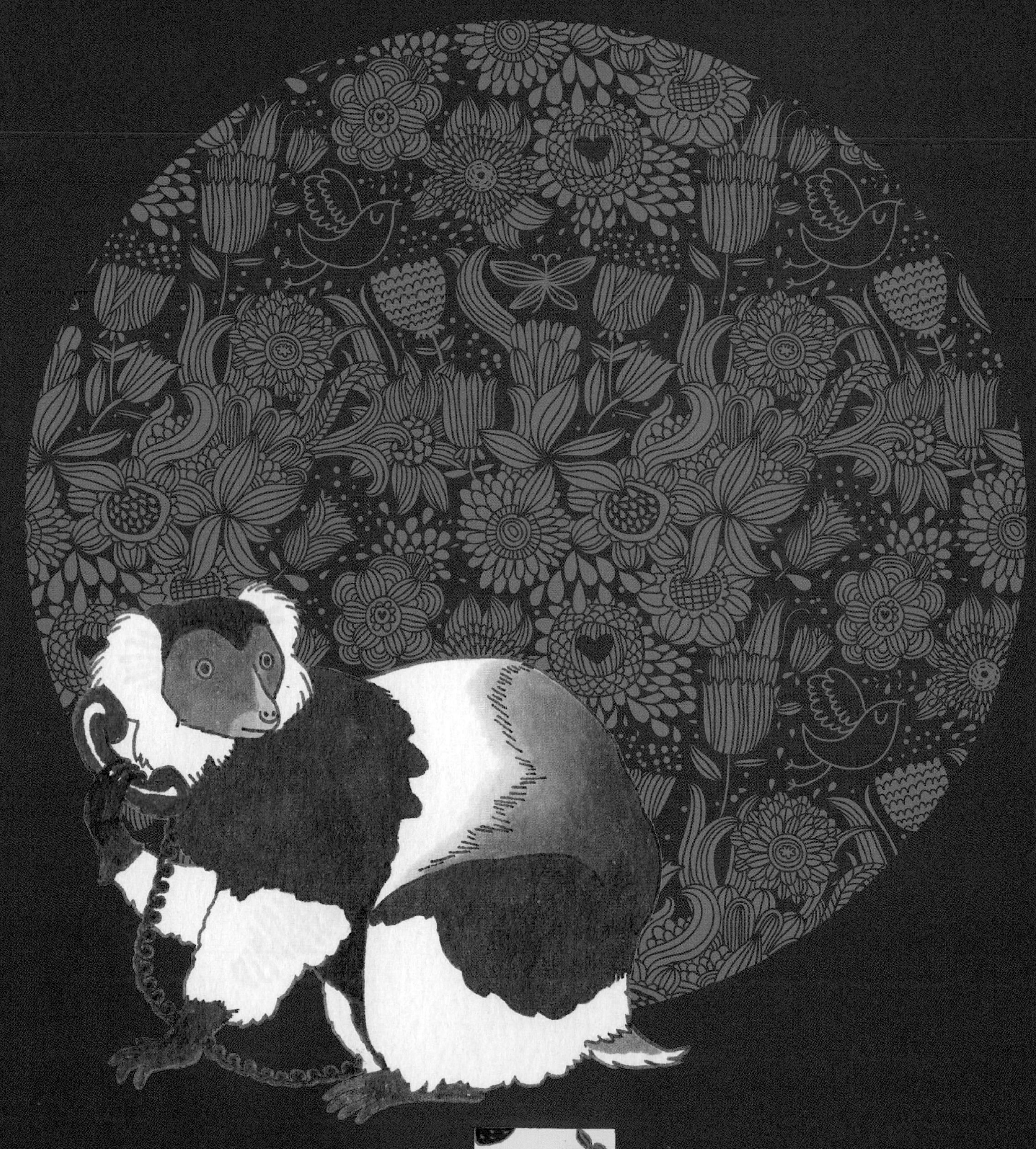

Indri

Jaguar

Koala

Llama

Moose

Newt

Owl

Pig

Quail

Raccoon

Squirrel

Turtle

Unicorn

Woodchuck

X-ray fish

Yak

Zebra

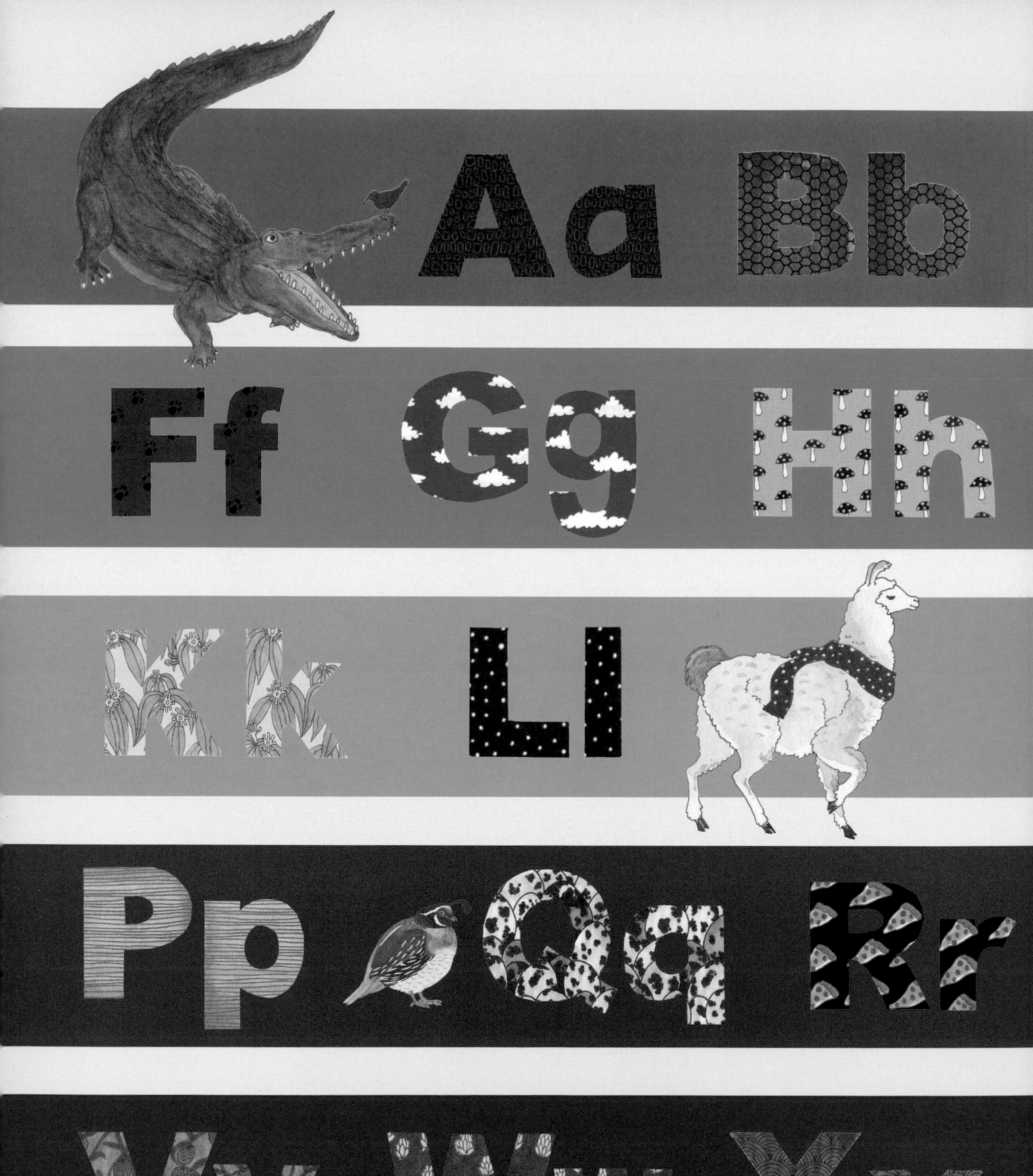
Aa Bb
Ff Gg Hh
Kk Ll
Pp Qq Rr
Vv Ww Xx

Cc Dd Ee
Ii Jj
Mm Nn Oo
Ss Tt Uu
Yy Zz

Aa
Bb
Cc
Dd
Ee
Ff
Gg
Hh
Ii
Jj
Kk
Ll
Mm
Nn
Oo
Pp
Qq
Rr
Ss
Tt
Uu
Vv
Ww
Xx
Yy
Zz

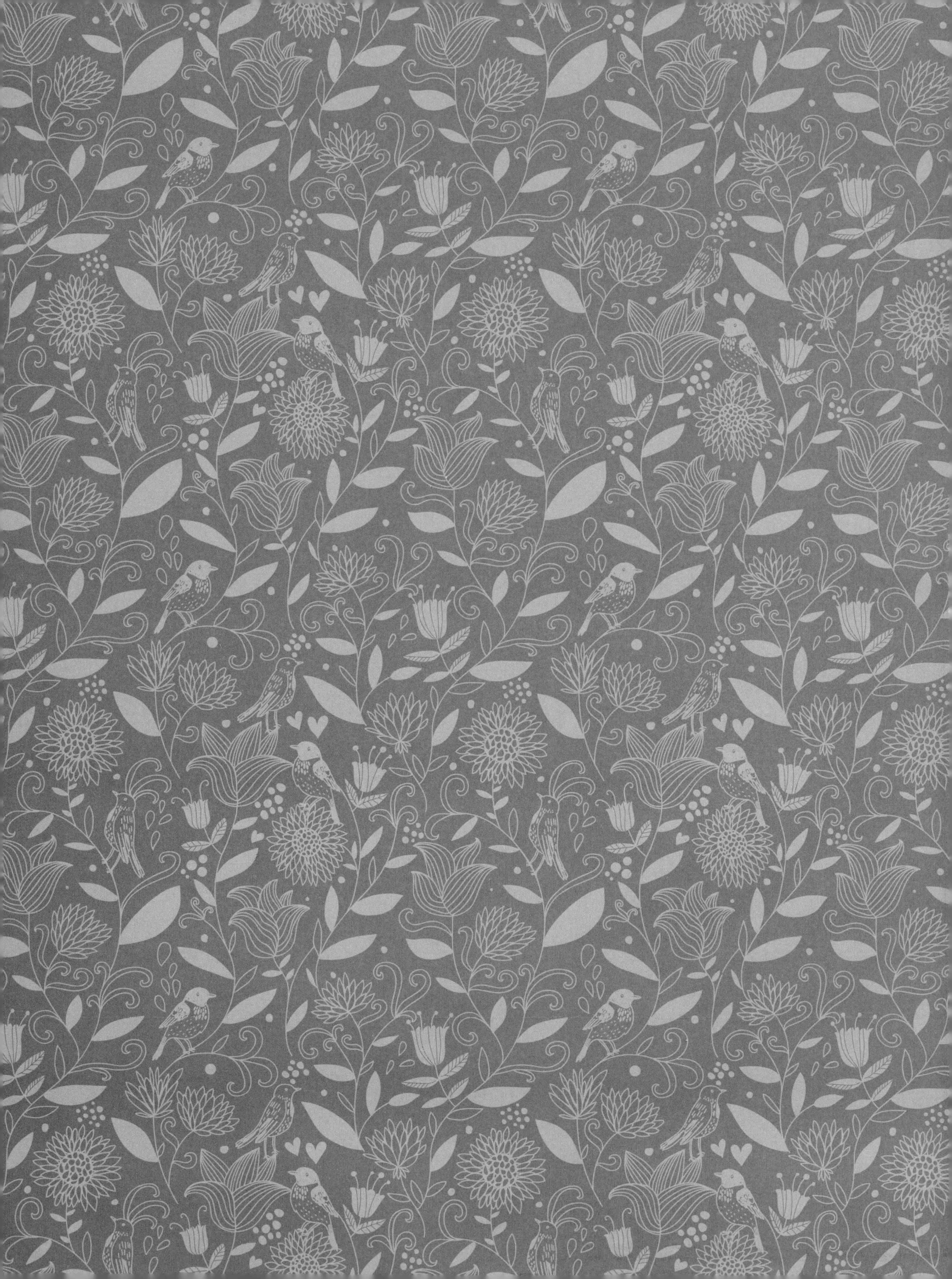